Hardcover: 9781736898703
Ebook: 9781736898710

First hardcover edition September 2021

Illustrations by Maria Finocchiaro

Printed by Ingram Spark in the USA.

#NormalizeGrief™

Grievingit.com

I dedicate this book to those painfully growing through their grief.

I pray this book brings you a little bit closer to where you desire to be.

Grief is hard.

And it sucks.

-Shanice

Grief on the Playground

Written by Shanice McLeish
Illustrated by Maria Finocchiaro

Summer vacation has come to an end. Ava is nervous thinking about going into a new school year.

She has been spending her last week of summer visiting her dad in the hospital.

"Coming!" Ava yells.

As Ava walks into class she overhears her mom and Ms. Johnson talking about her dad.

At recess, all of the kids are playing on the playground and having fun. But Ms. Johnson notices Ava sitting on the bench alone.

Ms. Johnson slowly approaches
Ava and asks, "Hey Ava, how are you?"
"I'm okay," Ava quietly responds.

"So, your mom told me that your dad died a few days ago. I'm very sorry to hear that. You know, my dad died too. I was 13 years old." Ms. Johnson says. Ava suddenly looks up towards Ms. Johnson with big eyes and asks "Really? What happens next?"

"Okay, let's picture a roller coaster. There are high points, low points, loops, and a lot of screams.

The roller coaster can represent how you may feel at any given time," Ms. Johnson continues.

"Let's look at the high points.
Here is where we may feel happy
or full of joy. When we are at our
high points, life seems normal.
For me, this is my happy place.
I know that I can breathe freely,"

"Life seems to be going well. You and your family are getting along, your grades are good, and your friends are happy. Now, it's important to understand that you are not going to be here all the time and that is okay," Ms. Johnson proudly shares.

"Next, the lows. This one is a bit tricky. This is where we could really feel sad on the inside. Let me tell you this now, this place is not the best... but it is necessary. This is where we secretly cry ourselves to sleep and pretend that we are not sad in front of others. We hide." Ms. Johnson continues.

"The loops come and go. They don't last long, just like on roller coasters. Here we can feel very confused about what is happening in our lives. Things may be changing: you may move into a new house, go to a new school, or worry a lot more," Ms. Johnson explains.

"A lot is going to change. It's going to feel different. But you know what? I see that you are strong and you can do it! You are not alone. You will have good days but you will also have some bad days. We are now on this roller coaster together, and I will be here for you." Ms. Johnson gently says.

"Thank you, Ms. Johnson. But when can I scream?" Ava chuckles. Ms. Johnson giggles, "Umm... absolutely every day," she says sarcastically.

"Thank you, Ms. Johnson" Ava smiles with relief. "No problem. Now come on, let's gather the class and head back in," Ms. Johnson energetically says.

From this day forward, Ava was no longer
scared to ride the grief roller coaster.

The end.

Printed in the USA
CPSIA information can be obtained
at www.ICGtesting.com
LVHW072042230823
756103LV00004B/6